GHOSTS FOR BREAKFAST

BY STANLEY TODD TERASAKI

ILLUSTRATED BY SHELLY SHINJO

LEE & LOW BOOKS Inc.

New York

AUTHOR'S NOTE

In the late 19th century, Japanese immigrants began arriving on the west coast of the United States. Many became farm laborers and later began farming on their own, and several cohesive farming communities developed. In the San Joaquin Valley, in central California, dozens of Japanese farmers established a Yamato Colony, or "New Japan." In southern California, Japanese truck farms flourished, producing vegetables for market. In the 1920s, my father grew up on such farms in Orange County and the San Fernando Valley. Long Beach, south of Los Angeles, also had a thriving Japanese farming community. As a teenager my mother worked at a produce stand where farmers from Long Beach sold their goods.   —S.T.T.

Text copyright © 2002 by Stanley Todd Terasaki
Illustrations copyright © 2002 by Shelly Shinjo

All rights reserved. No part of the contents of this book may be reproduced by any means without the written permission of the publisher.
LEE & LOW BOOKS Inc., 95 Madison Avenue, New York, NY 10016
www.leeandlow.com

Printed in China

Book design by Tania Garcia
Book production by The Kids at Our House

The text is set in Della Robbia
The illustrations are rendered in acrylic

10 9 8 7 6 5 4 3 2 1
First Edition

Library of Congress Cataloging-in-Publication Data
Terasaki, Stanley Todd.
    Ghosts for breakfast / by Stanley Todd Terasaki ; illustrated by Shelly Shinjo.— 1st ed.
        p. cm.
    Summary: One night, a young boy and his father investigate their frightened neighbors' report of ghosts on a nearby farm.
    ISBN 1-58430-046-9
    [1. Ghosts—Fiction. 2. Radishes—Fiction. 3. Japanese Americans—Fiction. 4. Humorous stories.] I. Shinjo, Shelly, ill.
II. Title.
PZ7.T2665 Gh 2002
[E]—dc21   2001038786

TO THE AUTHOR AND FINISHER OF MY FAITH,
AND TO NANCY — S.T.T.

TO MY BELOVED SCOTT, WHO TRAVELS WITH ME
TO SEEK BEAUTY EVERYWHERE — S.S.

PON! PON! PON! PON!
The pounding at the door shattered my family's peaceful evening.
PON! PON! PON! PON!
Who could it be at this time of night? I saw Mama's puzzled look
as Papa opened the door a crack and peered out.
"Ah," Papa sighed. "The Troublesome Triplets."

Papa opened the door, and Mr. Omi, Mr. Omaye, and
Mr. Ono stumbled in.

"Oh me," said Mr. Omi.

"Oh my," said Mr. Omaye.

"Oh no," said Mr. Ono as the three of them huddled
together, trembling. Everyone called them the Troublesome
Triplets because you never saw one without the other two,

and you always saw them with some kind of complaint or worry.
But I had never before seen them in quite this state.

"What is it?" Mama asked. "You look like you've seen . . ."

"Ghosts!" Mr. Omaye blurted out. "We saw ghosts in Farmer
Tanaka's field."

"Ghosts?" I said. "Real ghosts?"

"Yes, ghosts!" said Mr. Ono. "This afternoon we were fishing in the river. We must have lost track of the time because before we knew it, the sun was setting. We hurried home as the sky grew darker."

"We took a shortcut through Farmer Tanaka's field," said Mr. Omaye. "And then we saw them."

"Ghosts!" said Mr. Omi. "In Farmer Tanaka's field, dozens of ghosts, dancing in the moonlight."

"And these ghosts," Papa said. "What did they look like?"

"They were long and thin," Mr. Ono answered. "And white, very white."

"White," Papa echoed. "White and dancing in the moonlight?"

Papa pulled his shirt over his head and tucked his arms insid
"Did they look like this?" Papa asked. Then, flapping his
sleeves and howling, Papa began to dance around the room.
"*Wooooo, wooooo, wooooo,*" he sang.
Why was Papa acting so funny? After all, there were
ghosts in Farmer Tanaka's field!

"Well," Papa said as he poked out his head. "Do I make a good ghost?"

"You can make fun of us if you like," Mr. Omaye said. "But we are telling the truth."

"It is only a matter of time before the ghosts overrun the whole countryside," said Mr. Ono.

"Who knows what terrible things they will do," said Mr. Omi. "Please help us."

"All right," Papa said. "Let's get to the bottom of this. Take me to see the ghosts."

"Oh me! Oh my! Oh no!" said the Triplets all at once.

"We've had enough ghosts for one night," said Mr. Omaye. "You go. We'll stay right here and wait for you."

Papa sighed. "Very well. I will go to see these ghosts of yours. And just to show you there is nothing to be afraid of, I will take my son with me."

Me! Papa wanted to take me to hunt ghosts? I didn't think that was a good idea. But before I knew it we had pulled on our coats and stepped out into the night.

We walked in silence along the country road. All I could hear was the shuffle, shuffle of our feet and the chirping of the crickets.

Suddenly the night air grew heavy and misty all around us.

"What was that?" I asked.

"It is only the fog rolling in from the sea," Papa said.

"Only the fog," I said to myself.

Soon the fog became very thick, thick as bean paste soup.

"Papa," I said. "I can't see a thing!" I moved closer and took his hand. It felt warm and rough.

And then I heard it.

Woo-o-o-o. Woo-o-o-o. Woo-o-o-o.

"Wh-what was that?" I asked.

"It is only the wind whistling through the trees," Papa answered.

"Only the wind," I repeated.

As we neared Farmer Tanaka's field, I was gripping
Papa's hand as tight as I could. The howling grew louder.
WOO-O-O-O. WOO-O-O-O. WOO-O-O-O.
"Papa!" I cried. "L-l-let's go back."
"Shhhh! You'll scare away the ghosts," Papa
whispered as we left the road and began crossing
the field.
And then, through the mist, I saw something. It looked
like . . . No, it couldn't be. But it was . . . Ghosts!
Hundreds of them. Long and white, with horrible green
hair! They were dancing slowly in the wind. And we
were walking straight toward them!
WOO-O-O-O! WOO-O-O-O! WOO-O-O-O!

I shut my eyes tight.

"Papa, please," I begged, trying to pull away my hand. But he gripped it tighter and we kept on walking.

"Papa, can't you see them?" I asked, peeking a look. Who knew what terrible things these ghosts would do.

"Papa, let's go back!" I pleaded, dragging my feet.

I yanked my hand and all at once I was free. I turned and raced toward the road. I could hear my heart pounding in my chest.

Suddenly I heard a scream. It was a loud, chilling scream. I stopped in my tracks. Papa was screaming!

"Papa, Papa," I shouted. "What are they doing to you?"

When I heard another scream, I knew what I must do. I turned and ran back. Back through Farmer Tanaka's field. Back through the fog and darkness. Back to Papa, who needed me. Back to those terrible, horrible ghosts.

Papa screamed again. Wait. This sounded different. It wasn't a scream at all. No, it sounded more like a laugh. Papa was laughing?

"Ha-ha-ha. Ghosts! Ha-ha-ha-ha."

When I reached Papa, I couldn't believe my eyes. There we were, standing in the middle of . . .

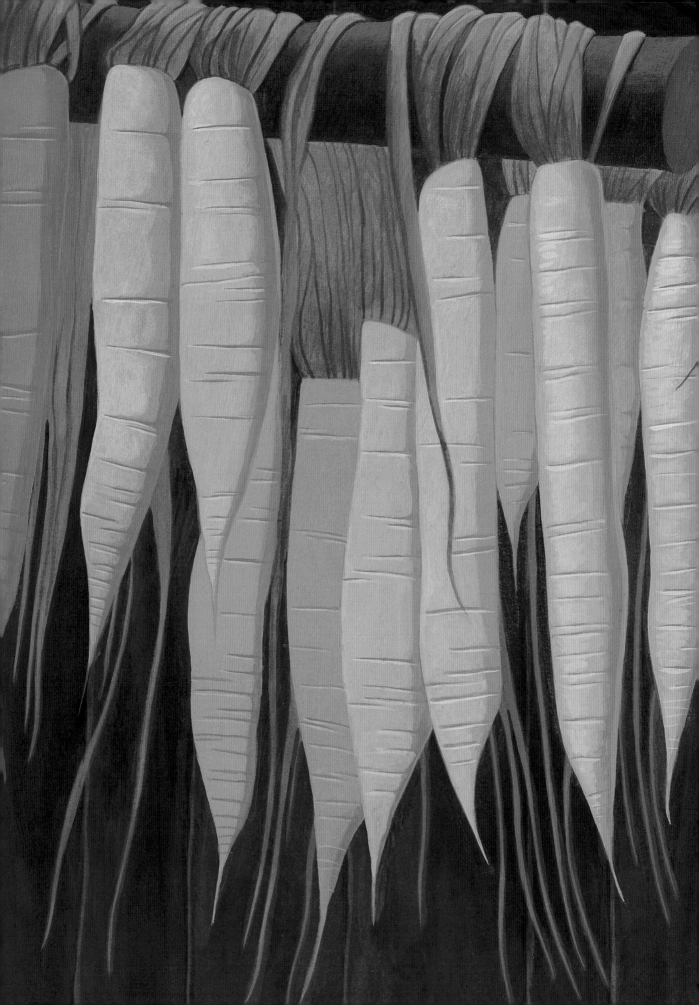

"Daikon!" I cried. All around us were dozens of long white radishes dangling in the wind.

"Wooooo, wooooo, wooooo," they sang.

"Here are the ghosts," Papa said. "Daikon that Farmer Tanaka's wife has hung out to dry. Just this morning she told Mama to come get some. They are ready to be pickled."

Back home I tried hard to keep the smile from my face as I entered the house.

"Oh me!" said Mr. Omi. "What happened? Did you see anything?"

"Yes," I said as seriously as I could. "We saw your ghosts."

"Oh my!" said Mr. Omaye triumphantly. "See, we told you it was true."

"Yes, we saw them all right," I said. "Not only that, we caught some and brought them home with us."

"Brought them here? Oh no!" said Mr. Ono, wringing his hands. "Where are they?"

"Papa has them outside," I said. "But don't worry, he has a good hold on them. They won't escape."

As the Triplets closed their eyes and slowly backed away, I threw open the door. In marched Papa with an armful of daikon.

"Here are your ghosts!" Papa announced as he tossed one long white daikon after another to the Triplets. "Ghosts! Ha-ha-ha-ha."

PON! PON! PON! PON!

A few days later during breakfast, we heard someone pounding on the door. Who should it be but the Troublesome Triplets.

"Good morning," Mr. Omi said cheerfully.

Bowing low, Mr. Omaye said, "Thank you for helping us."

"In appreciation we have brought you this," said Mr. Ono. He set before us a covered bowl wrapped in a cloth.

Mama unwrapped the bowl and lifted the lid. A strong sweet smell filled the air.

"Ah, pickles," Papa said. "Pickles made from the daikon."

"Thank you," Mama said as we helped ourselves. She took a bite. "Mmmm. Delicious!"

"Best ghost I ever ate," Papa said as he bit into one of the crunchy pickles.

"Ghosts for breakfast," I said.
And we all laughed.